Thirst

By

Addison Cain

Cover art by Simply Defined Art

ISBN: 978-1-950711-39-0

For James. Thank you for the hysterical
list of potential titles:
"Ink Me"
"Testicles and Tentacles"
"You Suck"
"Cling"
"That Left a Mark"
"1001 Hickies"
"Bound by the Alien"

Also, hilarious suggestions from Alta:
"Milk Mustache"
"Model Dairy"

Chapter One

"You know what I'm looking for." There was no inflection, no interest in the prospective buyer's voice. Straightforward demand and unveiled aggression were all Glabrx offered. He was not in such an undignified a pit for niceties—the best flesh market it may be—he had come for a singular purpose.

"Yesssss." Pleasure radiated from his lanky alien host, the gray boney protuberance of two digit hands waving toward the veiled display zone. "You will see this specimen is special. Set aside for one such as yourself. No other lifeform gracing Yarblock's Life Emporium has yet to see it. When rumor tickled my ear that a warrior of your species and stature might frequent my simple showroom, I had it set aside immediately." With a bow, the insectoid added, "The Cenoid race respects the Necrimata immensely."

1

"I am the first you've shown this to?" A shadow of appeasement led to the potential buyer's curled lip.

Traders could seldom be trusted on any word. The Cenoid arthropod might have dripped honeyed words, but it was money and rare collectables the Necrimata found on their hunts that often brought such merchants to slithering flattery.

"The fiiiiirst, yes," hissing clicks confirmed, the merchant's mandibles rubbing together, two greedy serrated fangs that *sang* when moved in the ugly fashion. "This one was collected recently, yet kept in sensory deprivation. This we did in place of *it* being fit with a control circle."

Glabrx was not a simple-minded buyer. His species were not kind, patient, or willing to deal beyond a very specific line. He refused to be led, swindled, or manipulated—things all too common in the Rpond Nebula. "A circlet? It's a sentient being?"

"The best vessels always are." The seller rubbed its two knobby digits together, stroking them up and down—fingering the bone, the round bulbous knuckles—hinting at what was to come. "There is more. This one offers a rare and coveted delicacy. You can use it for your pleasure"—overexcited mandibles clicked—"and feed from it."

Now that was something altogether intriguing. Eager to see what might lie behind the shining rare wool of so red a curtain, the huge warrior pushed past a squawking flesh trader. "Show me."

Fabric lifted, behind it a black energy barrier parting to reveal something unique. A vulgar display.

The upper half of the creature's body contained in a capsule, the being laid upon its spine, well fleshed, prettily colored. The bubble-like barrier around the pet was set so that Glabrx might look upon it, but *it* was unaware of everything outside the restraint pod.

Human.

The species was listed in the categories his kind learned after metamorphosis from larva to adult: mammals, restricted, base beings, *untouchable*.

Yet, this one… its lower extremities were free of containment. Very touchable. Ankles held in manipulation cuffs, legs spread wide, its limbs bent at the knee for maximum exposure of what parts the flesh dealer considered worthy of display.

The parts would be attended to in mere moments. What mattered now was the remainder of so rare and collectible a being.

Inside the containment, it looked startling. Soft, red filaments grew from its head, arranged on a pillow to highlight the structure of its facial bones. Skin that leaked no slime, covered in little more than practically imperceptible fine hairs. So near a Necrimata's build, but smaller, delicate in a tasteless way. This was no warrior.

Yet Glabrx's gums foamed venom all the same. Teeth involuntarily snapping from excitement.

4

Unaware, resistant, and mentally stymied, the flesh market dealer's catch lay still as floating jetsam, moving in natural waves to relive whatever motivated it to resist.

Arms stretched and bound, waist pinned by restraint beams, there was no part of its body the small thing might more than twitch in its wave. It was perfectly vulnerable. Visibly delicious.

So tempting that a trap was clear. "This is a mammal. A protected species… How did you come across one?"

The Cenoid arthropod clicked in its gullet, "It was acquired by poachers. My company intervened before it might be damaged. As collection had already taken place, galactic laws state it cannot be returned to its primitive home planet."

The lie was obvious, but in order for the human to be for sale, the ruling body of the quadrant would have had to mark the human as Emporium property. Otherwise, it would have been euthanized. Enough government tape had packaged up this tidbit, making so rare a catch truly available. And clearly, the Emporium wanted to be on excellent terms with the Necrimata to dare such a delight.

Complications…

Glabrx had not come to take part in dishonorable business, but if all was legal… "If I find out there is so much as a mark against my name in standing here, I'll see your entire spawnage crushed."

So deep was the bow. "I would not presume to implicate the great Glabrx in an illicit trade. Documentation has been filed, approval given to sell this human female as a Class One protected pet." Waving toward the exposed folds between the human's thighs, the merchant assured, "I guarantee, once word gets out, wealthy buyers will flock to one so exotic. Are you not pleased?"

That fleshy slit between the creature's legs meant nothing to Glabrx, but the scent radiating from it was delightful. Intoxicating.

Bending forward, the Necrimata warrior pulled aside his facial mask, exposed his jaw, and inhaled deeply.

That was the scent of... the ineffable. "Speak on."

"This rare prize is extremely special... not for general consumption or auctioning. It has been carefully prepared for many phases." One of the merchant's long, bulbous-knuckled fingers pointed to the contraptions encircling the fleshy mounds on the human's chest. "This female has been chemically roused to begin lactation. As you can see, light, stimulating suction has already been applied to lengthen and engorge her nipples. Her mammary glands are developing in perfect harmony to optimally produce."

The Cenoid arthropod's many feet shuffled over the floor to show another reading. "Should you be blessed, you might get that first drop to sample before your time here is up and the next customer is invited forward." Mandibles rubbing together, he clicked in awe. "Projections estimate copious output. Such a delicacy can be harvested at your leisure, enjoyed… even sold."

Perhaps not as tall as the lurking flesh dealer hovering over the containment pod, Glabrx carried three times the muscle mass. A thousand times the combat experience.

More kills to his name than such an insect might even imagine.

More well-laid offspring the Necrimata could easily inject within Cenoid arthropod weak exoskeleton to ease his unexpected seeding frenzy in place of buying *illicit* goods.

Crossing thick arms over his expansive and vibrant chest, the warrior scowled. "Can it be drunk from the source? The human, no matter your restraints, that creature is trying to wriggle out of our contraption. Such poor behavior suggests potential resistance. A Hpin Biped would stand complacent as I implanted it with a Necrimata spawn. You,"—Three eyes blinked, their vibrant purple irises contracted in the clearest warning outside of the lingering secretion a bug could not taste—"could be easily implanted with a Necrimata spawn so I might be on my way."

"Does not the hunter in you call for a challenge when you seed?" Unconcerned with a small show of disobedience by the human, the flesh dealer clasped his four long-fingered hands. "Where is the pleasure in complacent prey? As for the human's squirming now, there is some soreness involved as physiology adapts. Its nipples are being overstimulated. The light suction and squeezing manipulation accelerate milk production. Such discomfort is transient and unimportant. Optimal outcome must be achieved and behavior of this sort best culled through direct handling by its owner at the time of milking. Training—"

There was a series of beeps interrupting the merchant. Mandibles clicking in delight, the merchant gestured to the screen. "Ahhh, a new scan screen shows sweet fluid accumulating in the mammary glands. For the right price, this slave could be conditioned to produce constantly to please you. And in answer to your question, it can be trained to take enjoyment from the process, whether manual or mechanical. Observe."

The flesh dealer began tapping the controls. The appliance on the human's breasts kicked into life, pulsating in ripples around the entirety of generous, caught tissue.

Staring through the barrier, Glabrx watched the machine knead the girl's swollen mammaries, staring fascinated when the slave's lips parted on an exhale.

It fogged the glass, ruining the visual of such sweet smelling prey.

More clicks, more turning of knobs. "It is only a matter of manipulating the correct nerves. At your whim, its pain can be urged into pleasure." The tangy scent teasing Glabrx's nasal receptors sweetened, the merchant eager to describe the wonderful aroma when the warrior sniffed again. "Examine the slit between its thighs. Its genitals, *the human cunt*, are the reason this mammal will suit you in ways other livestock in my Emporium cannot."

A little pulse of the human's muscles set the pink lips between its legs twitching. The interesting sight, that second lower mouth, grew... moist.

A bead of intoxicating dew.

Breath sandpaper rough, Glabrx grunted. Each of the six tentacles growing in pairs along his spine unfurled. The appendages waved, stretched, and pulsed, no longer possessing the cerulean shade of a calm Necrimata. From base to tip, expanding writhing limbs took on the purple then red hue of an excited predator ready to hunt... or fuck. "Explain what I am observing."

The flesh dealer slithered closer, confident he'd hooked the attention of the warrior. "Unlike the single sex of a Necrimata, humans are either male or female. Displayed between its legs is the reason I know that out of all my wares, this *female* animal will give you the greatest satisfaction." A knobby, gray finger tapped a small, hooded protrusion at the top of the female's dampening slit. The captive jumped within its containment, squeaking out a note of obvious confusion.

11

Even so, that heady aroma amplified, those fleshy lips growing pink and engorged. "Here is their sex organ, a channel of warm flesh that can self-lubricate in anticipation of mating. Imagine it, Great Glabrx, this hot, slippery flesh surrounding your seeding flange."

From his spine, each tentacle reached beyond his massive arms and torso to sample the sweet place that now shined, pink and puffed.

And then he showed fanged teeth.

There it was, a tiny hole hidden between the outer lips. "It is too small."

Mandibles extended in the Cenoid's version of a grin. "This organ is designed to stretch if properly prepared. It could take the entirety of your flange with practice... kneading your wriggling flesh as its muscles spasm around you, taking your girth without damage to the host."

As if to prove his word, the flesh dealer pressed the tip of his finger past the pulsating opening. The long digit was maneuvered all the way to his first knuckle, and then for good measure, the bulbous joint, one six times larger than the finger, popped past the stretched lower mouth.

All of that bulk sat in the squirming human. And it *was* squirming, fighting its restraints, throwing its head back and forth.

The show was intoxicating. The smell a heady drug.

"Remember, since capture, it has felt nothing but the suction of its mammary glands and mechanical maintenance of its feeding and waste extraction. Many months of sensory deprivation has reprogrammed the nerves, adjusted the mind, and created an ideal physicality for ownership. The human is eager for stimulus. Look, its reaction is one of pleasure. You can tell by the flush of its skin, also the chirp from its throat." That finger pumped in and out, growing shiny. "Hear that song it sings? Beautiful, no?"

It was a temptation that Glabrx longed to experience—one that would cost a fortune with little return on investment if indulged in. "Once hatched, my spawn would devour this human's guts in a matter of days. There would only be one worthy mating."

"Aaaaaahhhhhaaa. That is the true beauty of why this specimen was set aside specifically for *your* needs." Pulling his slimy, shined finger from the human's mating recess, the flesh peddler demonstrated that the little hole went right back into shape, tight and small, and very, very slippery.

Mandibles clicked, the gray digit held up for his client's investigation, he said, "The pH of her secretions is acidic enough to prevent full attachment so long as the spawn is removed and preserved within a reasonable time. You could seed her repeatedly: train the human female to perform to your liking. It will *want* you to seed her. She'll beg for it."

The tip of two bright crimson tentacles slipped and circled the merchant's upheld finger. With each pass, a tingling sensation excited the feelers.

There was something about that human's juices that was absolutely delicious.

Trilling, the merchant asked. "Do you feel that? The acidity of its secretions increases your sensation. Imagine such bliss slathered over your mating flange. Human physiology can provide you with so much more than a simple vessel. Entertainment, pleasure, a pet to provide sweet milk at your whim…"

As far as Glabrx knew, no other Necrimata Warrior possessed so rare or reusable a vessel. If everything was true, great profit could be made selling his spawn back to the homeworld for training and service to the cause. If able to mate at a whim, his species would expand exponentially… others would desire a human. He could even rent out this pet for added compensation.

The use of human females could turn the tides of wars, populate worlds with workers. It might even have the proper genetics to enhance his spawn and produce powerful warriors.

And pleasure… writhing his flange in that tight, fleshy hole was a reward an honorable warrior of his rank deserved.

He *wanted* the human.

Two of Glabrx's tentacles impatiently butted up against the human's containment pod.

Accustomed to Necrimata aggression, the insectoid made the offer that would seal the transaction. "Great Glabrx, sample the creature yourself. One taste and you will know the price I ask is nothing."

To see the restrained thing filled with flange here, now, with a foul Cenoid watching? Already his mating organ had begun to emerge, flapping eagerly toward the scented crevice spread on display before him.

Whispering the enticement, the merchant urged, "Use the human. Sample its offerings. Specifics can be discussed later, and should you damage it, it can be repaired."

The human trembled in its pod, slit still flushed, nipples distended from the suctioning device. Eyes open, it stared up, seeing nothing. But its flesh had flushed a pleasing pink, its padded lips were parted, even its eyes seemed hungry for any touch, any sensation before sensory deprivation drove it mad.

The female had no clue what was coming for it.

Glabrx had seen it squirm at the knobby finger of the merchant. He had heard its squeaks from brief stimulation. What would it do when possessed by a ranked warrior with a large and hungry flange? Would it make more squeaks? Would its eyes flare and its mouth gape? More importantly, would there be any fulfilment in seeding a creature that survived rut after rut. Prey was supposed to die, be used for the enrichment of a spawn that would eat its way out of it. A true warrior's pleasure came from the hunt, the physical release from the mounting and planting an afterthought.

The triangle shaped pad of his flange began pulsating, stretching forward toward the nest of slippery human flesh the merchant had offered for the seeding. As he'd witnessed the Cenoid do, the tip of his engorged, veiny flange tapped the small nub at the top of the parted lower lips. A zing raced up his protrusion. It was as the merchant said; something in the human's chemistry affected the flesh of his mating organ. Pleasant tingles sent his flange to engorge until blood vessels stood proudly. This, and he had not even penetrated the creature. Fighting to control his thrashing flange, he slithered over and over the human's nub. The creature in the containment pod went wild. Had it been possible, it seemed to try to spread its pinioned legs even wider in invitation.

The offering was accepted, and with a warrior's growl, Glabrx's flange surged into that little crevice. Serpenting past the fleshy lips to burrow in that slippery channel, he found the merchant had not lied. All around his girth, the human's internal mechanisms were squeezing his accordion-like flange. Despite his prominent ridges and sticky valley, it was trying to force him out, the pulsating ring of muscles encouraging the opposite reaction. Deeper Glabrx stretched her, his hands slamming atop the containment pod. Every last tentacle held to human legs as they would his prey, entrapping each limb more securely than any manipulation cuffs might.

Aggressive grunts lead to deadly hissing, Glabrx sluicing through the human's cunt with force and delight. Each time the human squeezed harder, he flexed, expanding his flange from base to tip in a ripple of strength that made the trapped human squeal.

And yet that spongy pocket grew wetter. Unsure what was more pleasing to watch, his eyes darted from the flailing, contained body of his new pet to the place where its genitals were stretched and pink around his flange.

Filled as she was, that nub the merchant had tapped, that Glabrx had slathered with his flange, poked outward. It beckoned him to pinch it, a suckering tentacle slithering over until the nub was caught. The human's reaction was violent and immediate.

It screeched.

Around his flange, rhythmic suctioning pulled him deeper, spasms erupting the more his sucker titillated that nub.

In the seeding frenzy, the warrior roared. From the base of his flange it came, the parasitic spawn spewing down his shaft, expanding in a ripple of sticky sludge that burst from the triangular tip's singular opening. Within the vessel, the satiated flange began the process of attachment. Spawn, looking for a nutrient source, was nestled into a warm, wet, home of human flesh.

The seeding was complete, but Glabrx felt no urge to withdraw.

Flange hilt deep in human cunt, he caught his breath and found his pet doing the same.

"Do you see?" The merchant thought to interrupt. "Your domination inspired both mammary glands to release. A vial of fresh milk, its first offerings, is being collected as we speak.

Over the heaving chest, the nature of the attachment had altered. Gentle pressure was no longer employed; deep pulls of suction had caught up both breasts, stretching them upward as creamy fluid burst from the tip of swollen nipples.

The human seemed to notice, and where moments before it had smelled of pleasure, it grew to reek of fear.

Each breath of human emotion was intriguing, Glabrx anticipating it would flavor the milk perfectly. "Remove the sample. If she tastes as good as her cunt feels, our transaction will proceed."

The merchant was only too happy to oblige, his mandibles spread wide, his greedy heart eager for payment. "As you are such a noble customer, the machinery required to extract your spawn is my gift."

By the time negotiation was complete, Glabrx would have much more than just the pet and the machinery. The training of a human had already sparked a hunter's imagination.

Flange began to reduce in size, slipping out of a hole that, when closely observed, became so small, her fluids and his discharge squished out. It seemed foolish to waste it. Dipping his jaw to her cunt, Glabrx's twin tongues darted forward, gathering the nutrient fluid to be savored and swallowed.

Again, the human squeaked, her short breaths wobbling the flesh of her trapped mammary glands.

Oh, she would be amusing…

Chapter Two

Collection complete, back on board his ship, Glabrx had the sedated human tucked across his lap, held securely by all six tentacles for inspection. An injection had set it to sleeping before retrieval from the pod, giving him plenty of time to familiarize himself with the strange mammal over the three day trip to the Xerdic outpost.

Seeding frenzy riding him hard, Glabrx found himself mesmerized with parts of the creature beyond its mating recess—though a thorough inspection of that delicious channel would be conducted soon enough. Its hands possessed five digits just like his, but lacked a third knuckle and claws. Human nails were flimsy, this one's having been cut short to prevent self-harm. Atop its skull, long hair—a pelt as the flesh merchant had called it—hung, waving over his leg. Special soaps had been purchased to keep it shiny, all at great expense. Twisting his tentacles through it now, made him doubly sure the money had been well spent.

Compared to his hairless body, the female was different, soft, and covered in light fuzz.

Free of the milking machine, its breasts were bloating with accumulating milk. He intended to leave her that way. To indulge now would be to throw away an early training opportunity and a joyous domination for him. His pet had to be awake so he might stimulate it while he fed. He wanted to hear it squeak, feel it fight, and enjoy the first moment it would submit to his authority.

That didn't stop his twin tongues from lolling long from his mouth to catch the droplets the human's nipples leaked.

The taste was delightful.

At the brush of her flesh, the female grumbled in sleep, tensing momentarily then relaxing into the heat of its owner. Smooth, creamy skin changed, tiny bumps erupting over the surface—the cutis anserina effect: a sign of pleasure, euphoria, fear, or cold. Vasodilation brought a blush to her skin anywhere his hand stroked.

It was pleasing to know the pet would be unable to hide its reactions to his ministrations.

What simple animals…

Wrist tangled in his feeler, up went the human's arm. He bent the joints, manipulated the elbow to learn the creature's limitation. Until evolution favored humans, they would never have the strength of Necrimata physiology. Its knee bent the wrong direction. This female would be unable to jump very high, run quickly, or employ any sort of camouflage.

No wonder they were a protected species on their small polluted planet.

Chuckling at her limitations, excited by the prospect of exploiting them, Glabrx chortled with anticipated delight. He could not hunt his pet as he could a vicious beast, such an endeavor would bore him, but he could influence its thinking… make her mental prey. He would chase and corner this soft-skinned creature with his every action, all the while fucking it at his leisure, harvesting an army of spawn for the homeworld.

His flange flared at the thought, edging forward to prod at the human's belly.

The reaction was automatic. Glabrx could control an aroused flange about as well as a Beruse Wind Spider could catch a fish. Without intervention, it would try to penetrate the human's cunt.

Fucking limp prey was beneath him. A true warrior required his vessel to struggle.

Wrapping a meaty hand around the base of his member, he squeezed hard enough to disrupt blood flow. Flange flailing, in a course of minutes it withered back to a hanging, ridged trunk of flesh that refused to fully retract into his body. He laid it across the human's soft belly, smearing that tender skin with a leaking dribble of bright blue fluid.

The same blue had discolored the flesh between its legs, marking it as Glabrx's property. Seeing it had pleased him. Eager to view it again, his tentacles adjusted their hold, circling her thighs to spread her lower limbs. The flesh merchant had seen her bathed, but the spawn nutrient splatter had stained those soft folds. Using his forefinger and thumb, he spread open those vertical lips and inspected the layered folds of its sex organ. The female's nerve bundle was flaccid, the mating recess unlubricated. It seemed such a small hole, yet held amazing potential. Spreading her farther, testing the limits that slit might stretch with only his hands, Glabrx memorized all he found.

Pretty was not a word used often in Necrimata language, but it was the only fitting term for this pillowed slit. The stain of his excretions had only enhanced the cunt's appeal. It had even blended his scent with her aroma in a way that made him long to lick her there.

Remembering the words of the merchant, Glabrx twisted the idea into fresh territory. *"Feed from your pet."*

He could savor the tang of this organ at his leisure, fill his pet with both his tongues to gather the sweetness.

"It will want to fuck you."

And how did human's fuck? Considering the scent, the taste, and the feel of this pet, human sex had a likelihood of amusing him—though nothing would fulfil a warrior's needs like a rough and thorough Necrimata seeding.

Already he could feel his body developing spawn at an accelerated rate. This pet would be used over and over until his season abated, and then it would be leased to comrades he favored. The idea of watching another Necrimata warrior fuck his pet aroused his flange again.

Would it scream its song? Would it take warrior after warrior to please its master?

He could train it to do all these things. It might even offer rare entertainment to see the female mated by beasts and creatures of an equally exotic variety.

***

He'd carried it tangled in his tentacles for hours while seeing to his ship, a little limp human female burden. More than once it had grumbled, trying to move past the strong sedative. Glabrx had spoken to it, testing the translation mechanics implanted in the human's brain.

Over and over, he growled, "I am Glabrx. I am your master."

When the female felt the rumbling clicks of his speech, when translation had muddled through its dreams, she tried to touch her ears.

"I am your master."

He knew she could feel the warmth of his tentacles entwining her frame and kept each feeler moving to entice the human's waking. And then the single lids of its two eyes opened.

It woke as spooked as the Great Warrior had anticipated. Its drugged fight was instantaneous, pathetic, and thrilling. Irises in the shape of a feather gray disk, the overlarge pupils widened farther once focused on his visage.

A shrill, bird-like call came from its chest, dissimilar to the chirps it had made during mating.

His voice even, granular, and exacting, he said, "I am Glabrx. I am your master. You are my Class One pet, procured from the planet Earth and purchased legally. Do you understand?"

Lashes blinked over and over, the female shaking her head as if to clear it.

"The effects of sedation will end shortly." Watching drops of clear fluid drip from the human's eyes, Glabrx ceased communication and rolled his tongues from his maw. The salty droplets were tasted, the human screaming again. "What is this fluid? I did not read about it in the manual."

Hiccupping sobs, the female trying to curl in on itself, proved verbal communication was pointless at this juncture. Tentacles slithering to warm her trembling skin, he pressed the human to his chest and moved to immediately stimulate its genitals. Offering pleasure would teach the female it was safe near his bulk.

All six tentacles employed with holding her flush, it was the fingers of his hand that patted over the mating recess' fleshy folds. "Be an obedient female, and Glabrx will spoil his pet. Already I have made you sing female songs. Do you not remember how my flange, my feelers, came to you when you were in the Emporium's containment pod?"

It wasn't growing wet, the human's reaction to having its clitoris stimulated inconclusive. But it was rubbing against him while trying to escape, misfired signals in its brain leading to hyperventilation.

"Human cunt needs flange to remember this warrior's attention, or do you wish to go back to sensory deprivation containment?" Glabrx had purposefully only offered two options. His pet could learn its purpose quickly or be made purposeless and lonely in the dark.

Screams ended as she stilled, earning many pats from his feelers as a reward. A tiny, almost inaudible grunt at the back of her throat was her only noise when his finger breached the tight mating recess. Glabrx did not prod too deeply, instead, eyes locked on the human's gray irises, he pulsed at the gate.

His cautious stimulation began to reap a reward. Lubrication began. Soon he was knuckle deep in slippery tight flesh. "Good human female. This Warrior approves of your physical reaction. Soon my flange will make you excited, stretch you until your organ pulsates. Open your legs for me."

The girl had been staring at his vertical center eye, her attention fixed as if unwilling to take in the rest of his form. That had served his purpose, but at mention of his growing flange, its attention darted down, landing on the engorged, flapping organ. One look and its struggles increased.

Finger removed from its cunt, Glabrx wasted no time in subduing it. He gave his excited flange free reign. The moment it shot inside her tight slit, the female went rigid, back bowed, swollen tits pointed at his lips.

Two birds, one stone.

Sharp toothed mouth lowering, dual tongues lolling in anticipation, he took her nipple and sucked. A thorough seeding, a sweet snack, and a human trilling beautiful music as it wriggled, writhed, and clung… perfect

***

Crouched low, eyes to the rust colored floor, she trembled. Fingers pressing to her pussy, she thought to shield that tender place from the massive thing that towered over her.

It was not done with her yet. "You are to put your hands to the floor, pet."

Shaking her head no, Evangeline found herself too terrified to speak. Had it not been for the shade and texture of its skin, had it not been for tentacles aligned down its spine, it almost seemed human: two legs, though the knees bent opposite of hers. Two arms, muscled like a powerlifter. It even had a face, something like a nose, and a mouth full of razor sharp teeth. And *three* eyes. Two, in sockets like hers, one turned sideways in the center of its forehead. And unlike its purple brothers, it was pigeon blood ruby red.

"What I put inside you is my property. If it is not removed, the parasitic nature of my spawn will begin devouring your internal organs until it bursts from your soft underbelly to consume your corpse."

Sobs came to partner her tears. None of this could be real. It was only a nightmare brought on by smoking too much pot.

A tentacle slithered into her line of sight. Before she might skitter back, the flushed appendage circled her wrist. Caught, her hand was jerked away and put to the floor where the monster had expected it, upsetting Evangeline's balance and causing more of the gelatinous deposit in her pussy to splatter out.

Having touched herself there, her hand had been stained the same electric blue as her captor. Seeing it was unreal. "Please, God, help me."

The creature took a step forward, more tentacles patting over her skin. "I am not your God. I am your owner. You are my pet, purchased to service me as you just did. I am responsible for your care."

Heart racing, her vision swam. The tip of one of his six hideous feelers caught her chin. Forced to raise her head, she looked upon the beast.

Blue… an unimaginable shade of vibrancy warned that this being was dangerous. She'd seen parts of it change color to violet then crimson when she'd awoken and tried to run—most notably, that deceptive trunk dangling between its muscular legs that seemed to continuously reach for her

Before she might break free, those wriggling octopus tentacles had positioned her in the air, legs spread.

Grunting like a wild pig, he'd put that wriggling thing inside her and manipulated her clitoris with one of those awful suckers.

"There, pet." His hissing bark of speech was anything but soothing. "Behave and be rewarded with pleasure."

Sucker by sucker, he'd run over her nub, the sensation nothing like she'd known before. It was impossible to disregard. Even being rutted by a demon from hell, she had grown so aroused her hips had begun to move of their own accord.

"Good."

Good? The monster blinked at her, the two 'normal' eyes human in shape but pupils vertical and pink.

Groaning from the wriggling thing stuffed in her pussy, Evangeline tried to scratch the beast... to stop him from stuffing more of that thing inside her. No, that's not what she'd done. She'd grabbed at his arm to angle her body for better penetration, lying to herself that it was an act of self-preservation. Just like the grinding of her pussy on that expanding shaft of alien cock.

Evangeline didn't know who he was, where she was, how blue, then purple, then red skin could have the feel of a snake but the heat of a sun.

"Too much," she'd whined.

It showed its teeth. They were sharp and pointed, a pair of blood red tongues lolling out when the monster's jaw unhinged in a threatening hiss. No bite had followed, only the lap of her nipple moments before her breast was caught up in that foul mouth.

The beast had sucked… and it had felt good. She'd felt the burst of fluid leave her tit, somewhere in her brain registering that it must be milk, and found herself hoping he would relieve the other aching globe bouncing on her chest.

On that surge of traitorous thought, she'd been forced beyond the point of explosive orgasm. As waves of poisonous pleasure had overcome her, she'd fought. Once he was burrowed completely inside her body, the fight had been lost. Laying still, staring up at the hissing monster, those fat tentacles had touched her everywhere. One had even dipped past her gaping mouth to toy with her tongue.

Stuffed full of the freak, she had cum, and cum, and cum. And still the alien had used her. It had even laughed when she cooed against her will. *"You like being fucked by my flange, noisy pet?"*

Her shame, her terror, had twisted into one long wail. It had rewarded her *noise* of refusal with more pulling suction on her hardened clit.

At that, she'd spurt, fluid shooting from her body like a bad Asian porno.

The beast had not minded being urinated on. Instead, it grew frenzied and began to pulse inside her.

Through the ordeal, it had not fucked her like a man would have. There was little thrusting, it didn't need to with its alien cock moving, stretching, twisting, and growing all on its own. But he had bumped his pelvis against her pussy, rubbing her tormented lips with his shark skin bulk. It *wanted* to inspire her pleasure.

Now that it was done, now that she was crouched, looking up a something four times the size of a man, she could feel its tentacles brushing against where she ached.

Worried it would fuck her again, she said, "It hurts."

He answered her with a hum of noise. "You will learn to appreciate seeding discomfort over time. Adaptation is inevitable. Tiny human pet, you will be well cared for by this warrior."

It spoke in a series of grunts and growls, something in her mind translating guttural speech into English. The tip of his feeler ghosted over her lips, on it was a smearing of the sludge dripping out of her body. When disgust caused Evangeline to pull away, his seeming gentleness was replaced with force. Arms and legs entangled by tentacles, she was flipped to land on her back. Air knocked from her lungs, she gasped.

It was intrigued by the reaction. "Humans are delicate. Do not make me harm your body. It is an inconvenience to repair you should a bone break."

The thought that he might break her bones, fix them, and then break them again was too much to process. Evangeline went limp. Bloodless, she met the vertical pupils of the creature who claimed to own her.

"Should I seed you, once my flange has emerged from your cunt, you are to sit upon this device." Moving her as if she weighed no more than a feather, tentacles lifted her body from the ground and set her on the room's only chair—if it could even be called a chair. Mostly, it resembled a saddle.

It wasn't leather under her sore pussy, but a material that moved, targeting her genitals. Before she might shift away, it poked its way into her dripping vagina.

"Do not struggle, pet, and the procedure will go quickly."

Procedure?

Bowed back, legs splayed wide by insistent tentacles, the *chair* had complete access. Whirring, the machine penetrated deep, buzzed, and located its target. Where her belly had a little bulge, skin instantly convexed, and down her passage came something caught up in the machine's probe.

Expelled into containment was a writhing mass, greener than any jungle leaf and striped like a tiger.

As Evangeline gaped, her owner removed the *thing* and held it in his hand. "Human DNA flavors this spawn in a way I have not seen before. This shade of larva is unusual in our species."

That thing had come out of her! The alien had put it in her. "My God…"

Annoyance colored his reply, the alien deigning to glare down at her. "I have told you: I am not your God. My name is Glabrx, you may call me that."

The day had gone from terrifying to insane. "What is that?"

"Necrimata spawn, offspring in your culture. It is to be implanted into disposable livestock where it will hatch and grow."

He had said he'd seeded her. Evangeline coughed, gawking. "A child?"

"We do not raise our young as mammals do. Should it survive two years of larval life stages, it will be fully grown and harvested for society's enrichment." Seemingly amused, Glabrx pat her head with his free hand. "If your contribution is useful to me, I will reward you."

A reward? There was only one thing she wanted. "Will you take me home?"

Ignoring her question, the warrior outlined what she might anticipate. "Humans enjoy physical contact. I will pet you." He acted immediately, tentacles scooping her off the saddle to bring her to his chest. When she was cradled skin to skin, Glabrx began to rub her head. "There, tiny female, my body heat will relieve your shivering. Stay docile, and there will be food and a bath provided for your comfort and health."

Squished to his body, Evangeline found his shark skin warm and unyielding. He was too hard to be comfortable, especially against her aching breasts. Furthermore, having her head pat like she was some animal was not at all reassuring. She could not move, dangling naked, slime still dripping from between her legs.

Chapter Three

The tips of mighty tentacles played in her hair, deft enough in their movement to relieve tangles as aptly as any brush. It almost seemed as if the appendages had a life of their own, their owner paying no attention to her as he piloted his ship.

That first view of the cosmos—once her head had cleared of lingering drugs, lingering tingles of over-stimulation, and lingering fear had faded into an unsettling apathy—was stunning.

They were flying through the stars, a view that meant nothing to him but everything to a small-town girl buried in student loan debt, stuck working ever rotating temp jobs between night classes in an attempt to be *more*.

That strangeness also quieted her mind to a stuttering halt. This was real. The warm, hard body of the shark skinned, momentarily blue male alien *was real*. Earth was not in view, and when she squeaked out a question of why she could not see it, he had bluntly stated, "Your planet is so far from here that not even my ship's censors can pick it up."

How was Evangeline to feel about that? About any of this?

The shivering wasn't just from the cold. She was in shock.

And more than anything, even more than going home, she did not want to go back to the endless silence of that dark place where she'd hardly existed. That empty place she'd been left to languish in for so long. Had it been weeks? Years? Had she aged?

There had been no mirror, and looking down at her body, all she found different was the massive engorgement of her breasts. That still dripped milk and the occasional lolling set of red tongues dangling loose to swipe up the beads.

Milk! As if she'd had a baby.

Though, perhaps considering the activities of the last few hours, maybe those things that would eat her if left inside were *babies*. Larva, altered by her in some way. Special, he'd said.

Vigorous.

Green striped little things that ate their way out of a body and needed two years to become full grown.

The alien who'd fucked them into her had been quite pleased.

His body had been extremely excitable.

His flange—and that was the word he had used to describe it when that odd sexual organ began to sniff her out again: *flange*—was firmly in her grip to prevent more laying of larva in her vaginal canal. Like a wet, hairless kitten, it wriggled and squirmed, seeking both to be pet and to be free. But Evangeline had already learned that squirming appendage could not be trusted. It had one goal—like the tentacles playing in her red hair—it seemed to have a cognizance of its own.

A mission.

It wanted to be inside her, stretching, throbbing, doing things no fumbling boy from her small town had ever done. And it could make her orgasm in a way that had to be unhealthy. No human was meant to feel such overwhelming waves of euphoria for so long.

It was as if she'd forget to breathe, wake up dazed, her captor licking bright blue fluid from between her legs... with two freakishly long tongues.

The same tongues that darted out, yet again, to lick the dripping milk from aching breasts. An act that for him seemed normal and for her did little more than set her nipples on fire.

"I was tending the goats on my parent's farm. A weekend visit. I went outside looking to view the moon. There was light... just like in the movies. Aliens with big gray heads and scrawny bodies. And then, there was nothing."

Suckers slipping over her mouth, the blue alien warned. "No more talking, pet. You are upsetting yourself. Be silent, allow adjustment, and you shall be tended."

She didn't know why she said it, but out it came all the same. Silence was physically impossible at this point. "Humans need to talk when they are scared."

His head finally moved, shifting downward so that fixed attention left the flight screen and settled fully on her prone... everything. The tone of growls and hisses translated into a very clear attitude that he believed what she said was a lie. "That was not in the manual."

But it wasn't a lie. That's why psychologists existed. The very vocation she was hoping to someday achieve had she been able to graduate next year. Well, after another few years in a master's program raking in *even more* student load debt after that. "We are social creatures."

"The Necrimata are not." That, and a more frantic wriggling of his trapped flange, muzzled the last of her attempts to converse.

Until she dared break the silence again. "Are you going to kill me?"

Unlike her last statement, his attention did not leave the flight screen, though he did reply. "You were extremely expensive. A Class One pet—a protected species. You are also the first vessel I have spent my seeding frenzy upon that survived and gave me such enjoyment. So long as you always remove my spawn, so long as you are wise enough to behave. I see no reason you shall not have a long, comfortable life as my pet." He tilted his head in a very human way as if to consider before adding, "Though I can think of several scenarios that would inspire me to end your life."

A flicker of emotion and her heart skipped a beat. "Such as?"

"It would be wise of you to never shame me." Final, so final she felt those grunts and growls imprinted on her skin.

Though that statement could be taken in many ways, she had already accidentally urinated on him. In human culture that was definitely something that could fall into a shaming category. So shame to him was something she must learn if she wanted to live flying through stars.

"I'll need a better explanation."

"Do not concern yourself, fragile human. I will guide you." A sucking tentacle cupped her chin, lifting her head in such a way that she was forced to stare into that awful, vertical third eye. "But try to escape and that will be your finishing mistake."

At this his shading fluttered, blue in places skipping right past purple to red.

Shocked to see his skin burn bright, she released his flange and pulled her hands to her swollen chest as if safer that way. As if she would not be burned.

A clear mistake.

Now she had all his attention. "Only two phases in my care, yet the thought of you away from me excites anger in a way indescribable to a simple human mind." A ticking grew in the massive beast, more blue turned red, all the while the flange dug for it goal. Sneaking into the slippery slit from beneath her, moving like an elephant's trunk.

It burrowed in, stretching her, and seemed to settle as if yawning before a nap while it's owner blazed red. Penetrated, that thing wriggling to find the most comfortable spot, she lurched.

And when such movement caused the flange to hit on overly sensitive spot, she let out a gasp. "Oh God!"

Glabrx shifted his hips, thrusting as if in agreement with his uncontrolled appendage. "We have spoken on the topic of God."

Breathless, she squirmed. "It's an expression. I don't see you as God."

"What do you see this Great Warrior as?"

If ever there was a loaded question…

It should not have felt so good considering the ache behind the pleasure.

"A nightmare brought on by too many hours studying, too many joints on a rare weekend off. Men don't have flanges, or tentacles, or buy women." Though that wasn't entirely true, was it? Holding back a moan, Evangeline added, "At least not noble men. Human trafficking is only done by criminals on Earth."

What a sharp toothed smile brought forth from the massive creature— one fully red and salivating— it almost seemed to coo. "Insults from my pet?"

"Fact is not insult. What I say of Earth is true."

"You will serve a purpose, and this Great Warrior will maintain your comfort." The flange rattled.

"By constantly fucking me?" Which she was horrified to admit seemed almost normal in the hours since the first *seeding*. And the second, and the third…

"The warrior seeds when the warrior must. Dainty hands can only hold back an engorged flange for so long. And learn this now, pretty pet, agitating a

Necrimata never ends well for the agitator. But in your case, I'm offering restraint. The three spawn produced in your human fucking sleeve were all so exceptionally well formed that I choose to forgive you for the thoughts your statements inspire. Never run. Human meat is a delicacy on the black market—unlike the *legal* flesh market from which I saved you further abuse."

Eyes wide, body reacting in ways she could not explain, Evangeline squeezed down around that disgusting organ, pulsating and rippling as if to encourage that damn thing to do its worst. "I won't run. Where would I even go?"

"Nowhere that I could not find you and bring you back to my lap." The great beast practically purred, growing an even more intense shade of crimson, tentacles leaving her hair to position her physically so she might continue her internal massage on him in the most comfortable way. "The manual claims human nature is deceptive and disorganized. You will try to run." When her traitorous body squeezed around him again, so hard even she took pleasure in it, the male groaned, let out a long, sex-drugged sigh, before a burst of that blue fluid began to splash against her womb. "Even now you try to deceive me into complacency with such tricks."

Evangeline was not squeezing him on purpose, far more startled by what her body did than he was contented by it. And considering all three of his eyes were rolling back in his head, that was saying a lot.

Breasts aching, her hips ground down as if, like his tentacles, they had a mind of their own. The pressure, the pleasure, and milk began to run in heavy rivulets, sticky and smelling of subtle sweetness. It made a mess of her as she rode the very creature responsible for her view of space, freedom from the endless sensory deprivation that had driven her half insane... the great beast that would be the end of any future she had designed and worked hard to achieve.

And she came, from her own body's work, crying out, red hair flying back.

"My beautiful pet desires flange?"
That organ went from docile to fierce.
"Then flange she shall be given. No other
beast is quite so brave."

What had been the closest to
human fucking she'd thus far experienced
with this creature turned all alien, all
tentacles, all sensory overload and endless
orgasmic euphoria.

Blue squished between them, and
though she was sore, though her thighs
were bruised, though she was hungry, she
bore it.

Laid back on the flight console,
she bore all of what he might dump into
her, how he might sucker her skin, drink
from her breasts, and cry out praise when
that vile organ he shoved in her expanded
beyond normal proportions, twisted,
planted, and deposited a *baby* in her body.

A *baby* flavored by her.

That would devour her organs and
cause a horrid death if not removed.

He cried out when attachment was
made, held her a bit too hard. "How you

make my flange kick! A fortune shall be made off your fuck sleeve!"

The larva, huge and vulgar, moved down his flange as he birthed it into her body.

For the first time she *felt* what was in her. Not triangular tipped flange, but spawn. This one refusing to be still, already twisting too near her cervix as its little spikes dug in. "It hurts!"

Head hanging back, throat bared as if she was in no way a threat to so tender a spot, the beast enjoyed his bliss. "A strong one! For that you shall have an extra reward."

If that blasted thing didn't kill her first.

Out went that damned organ, a river of blue behind it. Evangeline pressed her hands to her pussy, refused to see her belly move as that thing inside her moved, and ran from the room to the special seat that would instigate removal.

The alien followed, crossing his arms and stretching his tentacles to see her sit on the extraction device and whine when the process was too slow. Evangeline *delivered* it. Saw it packaged for whatever was to be done with it. And saw no baby of hers in that thing.

Red was this one. Solid red with nary a stripe or spot.

No comforting green.

"You have made an elite warrior from my seeding." Patting her head with a great hand, he added, "I am pleased with you, fine pet."

Blue, so much blue on her fingertips when she slumped off the device and cupped her aching place. She had to out think this, to remember why tentacles and orgasms were tied to larva that *ate* it's laying place. She needed space to breathe. "I am cold, and I need soft things on which to rest. You are not soft. Where can I sleep?"

Dragging his eyes from his squirming spawn in its storage sleeve, Glabrx, had he eyebrows, would have raised them. "Your body requires heat.

This ship is too cold for your safety. You must always be touching me. My body is where you sleep, eat, and function."

"And pee?"

"Waste shall be seen to when your internal monitors alert me to such a need."

What the fuck? "I need a place to bed down. You might lie beside me, but humans cannot sleep on other beings." And privacy, she needed a moment alone before she went mad. "Or you might give me clothing? Where is the toilet?"

"Clothing?" Arms crossed over a chest so well defined, steroid users on Earth would worship his form. "Your form is appealing, and I wish to look at it. The state of your flesh is a sign of my honor. Others will see there are no marks and laud me. To cover it would be to tell the world I am incompetent. There will be no clothing for you, pet."

But bruises were there, between her thighs, and lewd as it might be, Evangeline parted her legs to show him. "I am marked. *Damaged* was the word you used. A fragile human. A Class One pet. Who needs a bed and a toilet!"

Fluid, legs bending backward, the creature crouched, eyes a lashes blink from her bruised skin. And then it rattled. Not only vocally. An earthquake like tremor went through all its parts, all its tentacles. Even the flapping flange coughed out a sad squirt of blue before retracting.

That fucking thing could retract! She'd had a strangle hold on it for hours, and it could retract? Not only was she bruised, aching, overwhelmed, and hungry, she was also pissed off.

Everyone had their breaking point and that was hers. "I want my bath. I want food. You promised to care for me! Am I not a protected species? I gave you an elite warrior?"

And all of her tirade was so incredibly stupid that on a primal level she realized punishment would follow, but so far out of her depth, all Evangeline might wield as a weapon against this beast was throwing his promises in his face. And adding on for good measure, she pulled her blue stained fingers from her pussy and flung his fluids on the ground, "Your manual is fucking garbage."

"Did you just use foul language in my presence, pet?"

Worked up, sweating, smeared in fluids, she shrieked. "My name is Evangeline, mother of that thing that was just pulled out of me. Mothers on my world are celebrated and adored!"

"Mother?" The concept appeared to throw him.

And it was there, the translation working however their tech did to make that name solid in the alien's understanding. "You would be mother to one of mine? Such a thing would kill you. Though you honor me in so deep an offering."

The translation between them was clearly flawed. "Mothers on my world are protected by their husbands or wives. Should a *larva* put them in a position where their life is in danger, the child is removed." Not a lie. Caesarean sections happened consistently for such a reason. But not a full truth either. "Mothers are given soft places to rest, bathed, and fed. Treated as equals by their counterparts."

The alien slowly going from red to purple, it was the first time Evangeline heard the true hideousness of an alien laugh—if you could call a series of hissing grunts laughter "Pet, you are no equal. None is equal to a Necrimata."

Why was this thing just as bad and men from her town, her campus, and her job? Why did it send her skin into an angry flush? "Your Class One pet wants to eat! She wants to be clean! SHE WANTS TO SLEEP ON SOFT THINGS!"

"Deceptive, pretty human." Stretching of those tentacles, all six reached for her at once, pulling her close to warm icy skin back to pink. "This concept of soft things… there is nothing soft here."

Voice heavy with everything, Evangeline mumbled, "I cannot sleep on your body."

"You'll learn, fierce thing."

"I need food, and I need to pee."

It smirked, fangs poking from a lipped mouth. "And both life necessities are at your fingertips, should you ask your master kindly."

Feather gray eyes in a pale freckled face looked up. Her wild, red hair was a mess, her body the canvas for alien *things* and stimulated by many roving tentacles. Self-preservation made it easy to beg. "Please. Please give me someplace soft to sleep."

"Luxuries you require? This was not in the manual."

Again with the manual! "May I read your manual? As an expert in humans, I might make a few notes."

There wasn't any indication he'd heard her before her eyes began to shutter, roll back, jaw hanging lose. *The manual* was being downloaded into her brain.

Foaming at the mouth by the time it was done, Evangeline hung limp in his slithering hold.

As if adding a note of his own, he stated, "Your brain is not evolved to the point of handling a simple information transfer."

Not that it would matter at this point, but she was utterly screwed. The manual was committed to her memory as if it had always been there. Much like his language. And it was wildly incorrect.

A cough, one that misted blood from where she'd bitten her tongue marked his face. "I won't survive you. Humans cannot live without water after three days; we need it several times a day just to function normally. This manual says water weekly by human time. That is not a way I'd choose to die. Fuck me to death instead. At least then when the end comes, it won't be after days of suffering."

And with that, she passed out.

Chapter Four

A pallet of soft furs. Waking snuggled on her side, over and under Evangeline's skin was cushioned. Her fluttering fingertips, resting against her cheek, were stained blue from alien cum. But she was warm, and more importantly, she was alone. Even sporting a view.

The entire wall was *open* to space. Either a projection or a window or *an anything* that advanced alien tech might have to offer so fine a vantage.

Stars in the extreme distance; closer stars zinging by. In a room that, in that moment, held space and the glories of the night sky she'd loved all her life.

And it was then Evangeline felt warm tears. From eyes they fell, to dampen the furs, though she didn't warble or wail.

She just leaked out stuck feeling, passed it from one space to another, and grew lighter as it drained.

Emotion returned.

Bedazzlement by the stars. Acute anxiety when she dared consider how she'd gone from feeding goats, to endless nothing… to this.

This was real.

She was never going home.

Her apartment she'd worked so hard to pay for, her unfinished knitting, her massive, never-ending pile of debt, her parents and the hungry goats.

Her cheap suits and smart blouses. Her love of Cheetos.

The unfinished puzzle on her coffee table.

The smell of grass. The nightly song of katydids.

Car exhaust. Car payments. Endless car repairs. Gasoline and riding the tank of her ancient Hyundai to empty.

Tuna fish sandwiches and warm, sun-ripened tomatoes.

Men who never called back. The abortion she'd had when a condom broke and her high school sweetheart dumped her.

Endless regrets. Endless goals.

Endless space out that window.

Stars.

Burning before her. Their light blocked by whatever mechanism served as a window, but she could feel it warming her all the same.

Heat loosened cold limbs, left her groaning in pleasure as she stretched on the softest fur human flesh might know. And just as soon as that sense of comfort came, doubt rode hard on its coattails.

Doubt rocked through her like a bolt of lightning. All at once, all too much... because she was human, and startled, and in a spacecraft. *She been repeatedly seeded* by a giant of a being that almost looked human but was so far from one, there was really no comparison. Which made her laugh.

The caught throat noise of a fracturing thing.

An Evangeline with a brain not evolved enough for a simple *information transfer*. Making her keeper all the more *God-like* and terrifying.

To him, she must be little more than a monkey who could sign and pet a kitten.

That must be how the horny alien viewed her. Despite her state education and her efforts. Despite her love of stars and goats and family.

Forget about a life of straight As. Forget the Master's Program in New Orleans she knew she had a real shot at. Forget helping people in pain deal with their issues and find peace once she'd become a therapist.

Forget and pin all her future on that view, those stars, the fact that life finds a way to survive even the most crazy of scenarios.

God, how her breasts ached.

"There is a species of wisp-like beings, beautiful beyond compare by the opinion of many. They flitter and move like wind. They laugh as they evade. No Necrimata has ever seeded one. Impossible to pin, evasive, deceptive, and also dangerous should they chose to lure you in with their delicious scent." Fingers she'd been utterly unaware of moved across her belly, a massive palm cupping slender flesh and pulling her tighter to the reason she was warm in the first place.

He was here with her. In the furs, its tentacles so still she had failed completely to notice she was caught in their net.

"You, tasty human, resemble such a being. Though you have been caught"—those appendages wrapping her flexed—"and pinned. The wisps too are classified as *social creatures*. Corner one away from its partner and they waste away in a matter of phases. They are like clouds; no flange can find an anchor in them. They weep. Yet still, it is a Necrimata warrior's challenge to attempt the seeding."

How awful for the wisps.

"But I have caught one, and she pleases me—though in the future she may try and fail to lure me to my death."

Sniffing, deeply embarrassed by the flush working its way from chest to cheeks. Reminded once again how superior this being was to have gone unnoticed for so long, Evangeline said, "We have a mythological creature on Earth much the same. A siren."

"Siren? A fitting name for a demanding pet."

"My name is Evangeline…"

"And you wish to retain it? Nothing else from your former existence will keep. You are not even speaking your born language, though you have yet to notice the change."

"Evangeline," she said with greater conviction, stiff in his hold despite the softness of the furs on her skin and the pleasing way every inch of his appendages stroked her.

"Evangeline, my siren. *Mother* to my spawn." Those words were given with what might be considered reverence, should a hissing two-tonged alien *warrior* be capable of such a thing.

And her silent tears dried.

"Glabrx." Tasting his name, rolling it on her single tongue. Awkward, staring at those stars shifting past, at a nearby ball of burning red fire, she tried. "Great Warrior and *father* to our spawn."

"*My* spawn…" Sharp teeth, gentle yet daring, took her neck in his great maw. Thoughtful, reverent, were his words despite his catch. "You are mother for moments only, the larvae you cannot keep. Yet, I have decided *you* are worth keeping. Worth wasting Hertlu furs which would fetch me a fine price. You have your soft bed, siren Evangeline. And now that you have claimed the title of mother and called me father, I wonder? Would you waste away if parted from me, social creature? It must be so."

A deep breath followed by a long, drawn-out sigh. "I'll waste away now if you forget to feed me."

"Faster yet should you lack water." He nudged her head with his, as if to show affection. "Other resources I paid a great deal for through the communication network of this quadrant confirm your claim was true. Eat, drink, and then I shall bathe you."

Burying her face in soft, white fur, tension eased enough for another full, rib-expanding breath. "Human women love warm baths."

***

An alien toilet was far different than a human one. Though the utter embarrassment of being shown how to use it, the various functions, the *purpose*… was.

Baths, even on a space craft, were literal.

Glabrx might have had a *toilet*, a literal hose that basically suctioned one's privates to keep waste product down, but he had a full, sunken—almost too hot to tolerate —bath.

A thing earned by a ranked Necrimata soldier, he'd told her. And with that decree, he'd puffed out his chest and made the tentacles at his back… *display*. All the colors, all very intimidating. Yet oddly appealing in their rainbow.

Easy enough to be impressed with a full belly of exotic things she was wise enough not to question the origin of. Easy enough when her thirst had been slaked. Easy enough when she'd been able to relieve herself.

Then he took her hand, so small in his extra jointed and very alien grip, and led her into the liquid.

This was not an Earth bath.

The gelatinous substance within was nothing like water. Hardly rippled, required a very bizarre cutting through of squish and pressure.

Yet… once Evangeline settled against the rim and *seeped* into the mass…

it was bliss. Comforting all the bits that ached. Working on her.

So much so that she lay her head back, let her swollen breasts leak, and saturated in a moment so comforting she may as well have been on a beautiful beach in Mexico under a bright, yellow sun. "Were there ever females of your kind?"

"Gender is not a variable in my kind."

Laughing, carefree with a cool cup of water to sip and a bath laced with heaven, Evangeline gave a single laugh. "But sex is all you want."

The gelatin swished, parted, and made way for the captain of the ship. "A true seeding frenzy is passed in a day, perhaps two—large, violent, intelligent game filled and left trapped so the larva might feed. That is what I sought at the flesh dealer's when my frenzy came several phases before I reached my favored hunting grounds. Yet my flange still reaches for you. My frenzy will not abate, only grows, wisp-thing. Mayhap I'll kill you after all. Mayhap knowing my spawn have been removed unbalances my species' natural impulse. You were meant to give your life for Necrimata young, not be enjoyed."

It seemed the creature tried to kiss her, acting out the endearment as if having studied the mechanics but never having employed it. It seemed to move like a slithering thing and cover ever part with every wriggling appendage.

It seemed to *appreciate*.

With easy strength, he parted her thighs, hitched them over broad hips despite the squish of the *water*. "It's the wisp in you."

"Your manual"—The very manual that came so much more clearly to her mind after sleep refreshed her—"states that I am a protected species. You must account for me to several governing bodies. You are not even allowed to sell me unless under very specific circumstances.

Every tentacle clutched, suckered, and left little circular marks where they roamed. "A Great Warrior of my stature grasps the need to serve their species greater good. After careful consideration, I intend to keep you, fill you, ride the frenzy until I no longer breathe. I will give the Necrimata much to remember me for as this siren pulls me under the waves. I will spawn a legion of young. Conquered planets shall be named for the sacrifice I pour between your legs." He tested a word, as if disliking the concept. "For the *babies* you season."

A ginger brow arched. Soaked and sated and suspecting some sort of sedative was in her water, Evangeline said. "And just how long will it take you to die of endless seeding frenzy?"

"If projections are correct, a hundred human years. Maybe two. During all of which I'll be unable to continue my duties or maintain my station as a ranked warrior." Flange began to poke about, seeking its place to rest. "Much I will give up to keep you, siren. Status, the glory of a different hunt, yet I will breed with you until I die. This I do for the greater good."

Laugher, glorious in its hysteria, broke free. "You will give things up? My life was stolen! A life that will not extend as long as two hundred years. Humans die around sixty."

Especially humans laboring under debt their whole lives, then laboring under ideals, then laboring for others, then laboring to pay a mortgage, then laboring to feed a family, the laboring to please a mate.

Only the disengaged, ultra-rich, or extremely rare person lived longer.

The alien nuzzled her temple, sinking even deeper until they were chest to milk-swollen chest. "I would never have handed over such treasures to a creature that was not modified. You are licensed and guaranteed. Full of nanobots to fix damage, genetically cleansed, fortified against disease. A thousand years at least you'll live. Chromosomal abnormalities are repaired as they occur. Your set expiration date was aligned to my life expectancy." The creature tapped his chest where the human heart would beat. "When I expire, you'll pass into the beyond, siren pet, with me. Tens of thousands of our children conquering the stars."

An eternity of being fucked and fed and bathed and laid to rest on soft furs. Sarcasm colored her reply. "How romantic…"

Thoughtful, the slither of his tentacled grip, the stroke of his massive hands through that gelatin, grew possessive. "Chapter three. The human concept of love."

Choking on the word, Evangeline squeaked, "Love?"

"Yes. This is fitting to such an unbreakable union now that the wisp-beauty is mine. You will love me."

So much for the Jell-O bath and opening her hips to the stroking of the triangular tipped flange. "That is not how love works, alien. It requires mutual respect, sacrifice, desire, attraction. You *bought* me! Nothing you might do would earn my love!"

From his smirk, those sharp teeth, the quick flick of his tongues over his bottom lip, the beast seemed impressed. "Ah, how clever the flesh dealer in his trade. There is a chase after all."

Flange went from seeking and playful, to penetrating and greedy. Leaving Evangeline bowed, fucked in all the *right* ways. In every terrible wrong way. Crying out to the glowing ceiling of his ship, she struggled not to reciprocate like a trained pet. *A mist-being.*

And already she felt a hunger, an addiction, for what would burst down his shaft, stretch her past pain, and fill her with a flesh eating *baby.*

A fizzle—a warped, bent thought. Touch she was starved for, this thing would give it. Rest she desired with a desperation that consumed rational thought. The ease of financial burden. The offer of two hundred years despite the gap in her front teeth or the dimples in her thighs.

How it already clung to her, spoke to her.

How it desired a chase. Back home, the men chased when the wanted to get their dicks wet. They didn't exactly stick around, and on many levels she knew it was because her attention was on her future. On escaping her small town. On achieving.

Being pleasured and served by this thing, despite the title of pet, was so far from anything she might have imagined, it almost seemed appealing.

She was a psychologist's wet dream.

"You will love me. The warrior in me knows this. You will adore me in your human way; I will give you every reason to do so. I will die young for you, wisp. I will spend my years fucking you into oblivion. Already you crave. That is nothing to what will exist between us in fifty phases. In five thousand phases, I imagine a palace will be granted on my homeworld just for our couplings. Enough fresh spawn pulled from your loins to blot out the stars."

"I do not love you," all said as ankles magically locked behind the creature's spine.

"Do you find me handsome?"

"Hideous."

"Said like a true wisp. How I will be envied!" Not a word said without reverence… as if this flesh devourer, this nonsocial species, understood the concept of desire. "Human mothers expect love. Thus it must be given."

The beast pressed her body against the edge of the oval depression.

"As do human pets." Evangeline sunk deeper, gelatin teasing at her lips as his flange worked, his hips dug, and her insides went mad. "Otherwise they are taken away from their owners and the owner is imprisoned." For flair she added, "Ownership is sacred. Curses fall on those who betray so an important a trust."

Without parting her lashes, she felt it, his stiffening, the subtle slowing of the flange, and alien evaluation. "Curses?"

Lifting red lashes, Evangeline looked at the monstrosity fucking her in his bath. "Of the worst sort."

"Lies."

"Check your manual. Section 47.2 Human Pets."

Three eyes blanked for a moment and seconds later refocused, the maw beneath it working its jaw. "I will give you nothing but the best, *mother of warriors*, pretty siren pet, Evangeline, so long as you season strong young."

It could not be as easy as this. Life had made that clear enough. "I will want to go home. I miss my parents and friends."

"You will be too impressed to consider that rancid place or the life you will never return to. Rest is with me. Soft things you demanded and were given. A bath to wash my fluids from your fuck sleeve and heal your hurts, you enjoy even now. What male on Earth would provide better?"

An appallingly excellent question. Deeper she sank into the goop, her mind unraveling enough in the madness of all of it to be honest. "That is so vulgar. It's called a vagina."

"I have an affinity for your *vagina*. It shall be available to me always. Ten spawn a phase." He thrust, as if reading the chapter on human sex and adapting to draw out his concept of *love*. "Twenty!"

"Husbands on Earth are not allowed to access the vagina without asking. That is how the best babies are formed."

Sloshing through the mire, tentacles trailing over every sensitive part of her, "Give me elite warriors, delicate, pretty mist siren. Ride me as you did on the bridge. Understand my affinity, knowing what you can provide my species will bring you honor. But do not try to manipulate your master. When I wish to seed, you will be seeded. Society needs all levels of service. I will sacrifice and so shall you."

Pulling her thighs farther apart, crushing her leaking tits, Glabrx's flange flopped and wriggled. Pulsated and leaked.

As if a human man, he fucked her as she lay back against the rim. Evangeline's eyes drifting closed, her body lax and unnaturally accepting.

He fucked her while this magic bath knit her back together.

He fucked her as he tried out Earth words soaked up from an out of date manual. "Darling, sweetheart, mon amour." All languages, all tenses, all falling from a sharp toothed, drooling mouth with tongues that lapped at her tits and a throat that hissed out ugliness.

And he came, however his kind did. With a war cry, with a grouping of sounds she could not decipher.

Thrashing, his spawn worked its way down the tube of his flange. Spat from the tip that then worked hard to burrow it behind her cervix.

She screamed.

It was not a scream of terror.

The child made that moment, made upon the pitch of a scream so sharp it sent her lover reeling back was white as fresh snow, with a bright blue line straight down what would one day be a spine.

After collection, Glabrx looked over the squirming thing in its containment bag. "I don't know what this means."

Lacking the bulk of its red brother. It had not bit and tossed about. It was steady, as if listening. As if coherent despite its lack of ears or eyes. Sweaty and spent and utterly unraveled, Evangeline panted into the air the strange thought that crossed her misfiring mind. "That one is a holy man."

"Yes." A great, solemn nod. "A dream reader. Give me more of these, *my love*, and the Necrimata will kill in your name. *Evangeline*.

Five more times he fucked her before she slept on the softest of furs, held to his heat in a ship that was ice cold. Green, red, gray, blue, white.

A different kind of red came from her canal the next phase, released by the machine as Glabrx drained her breasts.

A human period. A thing he took great pleasure in drinking down in the most disgusting of ways. Smearing his maw in her fluids, performing a fucked up version of cunilingus with two tongues and constant physical attention.

She was his favorite snack.

That was to be his game.

Milk was never for the spawn, only him. Only if she begged he take it, or as he gulped in the act of seeding her *fuck sleeve*.

Only if she raised her breast to his maw.

Then he slipped in his frenzy, twin tongues lolling, a great mouth sucking her dry when he was at fever pitch.

He was going to fuck her and drink her to death.

Epilogue

792 human years later

"You lied to me when you claimed two hundred years." On her shoulders hung a robe spun from the hair of beasts killed by green spawn, offered to their *mother* when they burst from their larval form and sought out their tribe. On the walls of her many rooms hung the heads of great beasts, disgusting things terrifying to behold. Those were gifts by the red offspring.

Every shade served their purpose, all equally important, all necessary to the expansion of the Necrimata.

Evangeline had shined surfaces, projections, mirrors, gems the size of people in which she saw that no single line of age had come in all this time.

Her family was long dead, Earth strange and dying according the reports she requested and was always granted.

Spawn seasoned by her body thrived.

Planets were indeed named for her. Warships named for her Great Warrior.

The human pet, once a novelty, was now coveted and guarded so her Glabrx could continue to fuck her. Wasting away over almost a thousand years as he gave his very life to put more in her. Above all, he kept her happy. Learned the concept of human joy. Claiming it created the finest offspring. But she knew, secretly, he too had joy in their strange union.

Had the flesh dealer known how he'd armed so aggressive a species, never would he have sold her. The Necrimata might not have yet blot out the stars, but several system had fallen to the new wave of life. Many quadrants were now theirs.

And though Evangeline never saw proof of another human female when she roamed her rooms or the city in which she was lauded, she knew, as any thinking being would know, that somehow this species—honor bound as they were—collected every one they might *find*.

"You lied to me, Glabrx." How long had it been since she'd cried? And eternity, a hundred human generations? She cupped his maw, turned his face to hers as they lay in her furs. "Two hundred years… Instead, for almost a millennia, you have given me more happiness than I might have ever imagined."

"Your attention kept me potent." Gray now, withering in these last few phases, his skin flaked, and his vigor drained. "Your love is more powerful than your wisp deceptions."

Old, he was. His full lifespan achieved despite his constant deposits of life against her womb. Yet, she was still young, with many, many offspring that guarded her like a treasure. And a fleet of potential Necrimata vying for the chance to take her into their care once the Great Glabrx faded away.

More tears fell. "I cannot live without you, my love."

In that palace, with their children, as violent and strange as they still were. As attentive and giving and utterly bizarre.

"I was commanded to hand over your life key." Wheezing, growing all the more gray, Glabrx sunk more into his dying frame. "So you might continue your mission with Konjil."

Kissing his ridged forehead, Evangeline snarled, "You wouldn't dare."

"I find myself incapable of sharing, even when our young come to see you. I hate them when they dare approach, wisp beauty." Death began to cloud purple eyes in sunken sockets. "Another shall not have you, for I know such a thing would make you unhappy. Even in the afterlife, we remain as one."

The last of his breath left a chest aged and molting, his final words to a being he'd whispered to in the dark as gentle as her simultaneous end. "I think I truly understand love…"

As his life faded, hers did in tandem. Her life key deactivated.

Evangeline draped over his form, a sweet smile on her lips.

And thus they were buried, and thus they were remembered. Statues of their final moments erected on all planets the Necrimata controlled.

I hope you enjoyed this special bit of fun! Thank you everyone who read THIRST and wriggled with all the tentacle action. Want more tentacle action? Turn the page for a taste of STRANGEWAYS

Strangeways

Chapter One

Cliché as it was, I set a cigarette to my lips and struck a match. The quick scent of sulfur, that beautiful moment of burnt wood… then first inhale singed the back of my throat. Nicotine laced smoke swirling through my lungs. Dark air. Dark thoughts. Out of practice, aware that my actions were foolish, the taste of tobacco was no longer one of pleasure as it had been while clubbing in my twenties.

The cheap menthol tasted flat, dirty even.

It tasted exactly how I felt.

The crumpled pack had been going stale in my nightstand drawer for over a year. Couldn't tell you why I'd never chucked it. Maybe I liked the accessibility to a frivolous, expensive pleasure. Maybe I was just lazy in the small spaces where I could afford to be.

I suppose it was providence—there I was, sitting at the end of my sex-mussed bed, sucking on a cancer stick… because.

"Explain to me why your back is to me and a cigarette is in your mouth." Such a soft voice: velvet on the ears—almost a physical sensation to hear.

I exhaled, monotone, and watched the sorry puff of smoke add to the already unpleasant smells lingering in the dingy square of my room. "It's a human post-coitus ritual."

"No, it is not." I heard *him* shift behind me, as if he contemplated edging closer before changing his mind. "It is a formula used in your media to visually style the end of good sex. Should I interpret this act as a sign you were pleased with how I fucked you? I would prefer to be told in other ways that do not cause harm to your body."

Sucking smoke into my mouth, swirling it with a tired tongue, I puffed my cheeks and let it free. A fake inhale. A mutiny.

Which, in its small and stupid way, felt *necessary*.

But he meant well. He must have.

Sometimes it was difficult to tell if the 'new species' were using earthling cues properly. Was he sincere? Did that dusting of hurt in his vocalizations mean anything? Or was he using the manipulations earth men so loved to pepper through their words to garner praise?

How did one even describe sex with these… *men*? "I enjoyed it."

"You don't smoke." The softest rabbit fur, the most lovely of spine tingles. "This is not a habit that is healthy, nor is your current action offering you a sense of joy in this moment."

How the fuck would he know if I smoked or not? Not that it was any of his business…

One last drag. A real, proper inhale. I let burnt air roll around inside me, all the while holding back a building cough. Dropping the cigarette into a cloudy glass of water that had been left for days on my dresser, I exhaled the plume. Watching it shift from strong gray mass into tendrils that twisted into nothing.

The darkened air dissipated almost as quickly as my comfort with this situation.

Cutting a shy glance over my shoulder, I forced a pleasant smile. The same one pasted on my face day after grinding day at work. It failed almost as soon as it was born.

One look at him…

Sprawled, utterly naked, propped on an abundance of cheap, mismatched pillows, he waited.

Sure, I was naked too, and he had a great view of the seated top of my plump ass and tapered back, but I was ordinary. Regular.

Normal.

This *man*… lounged, utterly unreserved, blatant in his sexuality. Brazen.

Where some kook had come up with the term 'little green men' to describe his race I'd never understand.

There was nothing little about any of them—not height, not build, not, um, *their parts*—that warranted the diminutive term. The specimen taking up the entirety of my bed was pure muscle, yet lacked the bulk one might imagine came with such strength. There was leanness, definition, in shoulders that were too broad for a human and waist too narrow. Over all that strength was silvery skin, though it did favor green. And just like us humans with our freckles and personal features, there were random defining marks that set him apart from the others of his kind.

Phi had stripes.

Those markings had caught my eye from the first moment I saw him reading a menu at one of my tables. Few and far between, angled to highlight his bone structure, those stripes reminded me more of sexy 1970's David Bowie than any of Earth's exotic animals. The most striking, *my favorite mark*, was a line bisecting his face straight down the center. Down his throat, and now that I'd seen him *au natural*, led to the treasure between his thighs.

"Emily." God, the way he spoke my name was a caress.

He was chiding me for my reticence, for my failure to meet his gaze… and I'd always been a sucker for guilt trips. Up went brown eyes, my attention all his. "Yeah?"

His toes—well, they were similar to toes—brushed my thigh. "Come here. Human women are to be attended to after they have been mated. It is mentally unhealthy for you to draw away."

It wasn't intentional, but I smirked. Phi had a knack for making me do that. "Is that what you've been told?"

Like running water, his tone could be so smooth. Placid, welcoming, *urging*. "We've observed your species for many years."

Shifting onto a hip, I lost my train of thought, a new one smashing in so hard my eyes clenched, my mouth went into a line. I grew tense.

Incredulous, I asked, "You observed humans fucking?"

"How else were we to assure we satisfied? Human females are far more frightening than the males. You must be conditioned to find us enjoyable, or we might be overpowered." As if utilizing a practiced expression, he winked. Hand to God, the alien winked.

And heaven help me, I giggled. I even put a hand over my lips like some sad flirt at a club.

But amusement faded in an odd and unmerciful way. I grew uneasy with the way he stared.

Mouth dry as a smoke-scarred desert, I fought my tongue to say, "You forgot to mention that we find you overwhelming and scary."

Phi blinked his second eyelid, a quick flash of horizontal movement snapping shut over fully black eyes. Like the shutter of an old camera snapping away, those peepers were always active.

Click, click, click, click, click.

There may have been no sound, but when he looked at me, I felt as if he was cataloguing, memorizing every twitch with a mental snapshot. Those upturned eyes seemed a mechanical afterthought of evolution.

Designed to be alluring.

After all, the entirety of him was enticing—the smoothness of his skin, the silvery-green coloring, the slightly oblong skull, even his practically human mouth. But the eyes… they made me feel as if I was a human living on a planet swarming with aliens that should not have been there.

Phi might look mostly human, but shit like that was a quick reminder that these new citizens were not one of us.

Like a languid stroke upon a treasured pet, his voice passed over and through me. "Do not feel fear toward me, Emily."

And with easy words from a lounging tiger, I didn't.

It dissipated just like my last exhale of that disgusting cigarette, fading into calm, steady air.

Still, I spoke of why. "Your kind just showed up here—legions of you—and no one said a thing. Our government, which I will openly admit is populated by warmongering idiots, just stood there, smiling, *waving*, as if they'd sent out invitations to tea. You live in our cities, you even dress like human males now…"

Phi finished my thought, the entirety of his expression gentle. "And the males of your own species are wasting away—have been dying off for generations. The majority cannot survive past forty Earth years and soon will be gone."

Exactly.

And how was it that such a phenomenon was something everyone noticed but nobody talked about? "My brother, he's thirty-eight. He started coughing last year… Tony won't make it to forty."

And while my brother could no longer work to support his family, I was here, having just let an alien fuck me until I'd come so hard I'd torn my cheap covers to shreds.

No longer willing to wait for me to lie beside him, Phi leaned the glory of his upper body forward and reached for me.

Pulled into the cradle of warmth, a defined and powerful chest to my back, I found his touch far more soothing than I should have... considering he was practically a stranger.

His ribs expanded in a great breath, arms closing more firmly around my much smaller frame. He even pressed his forehead to my crown before he said, "Settling on this planet was done peacefully. Not one of your species was harmed. There has been no violence. So, sweet Emily, please tell me the basis of your fears so that I might erase them."

My concerns were so straightforward I could not believe I had to explain. They should have been the concerns of every human. Even thinking of that day their ships blackened the sky, I felt my heart pick up speed. "The atmosphere burned, a wave of massive ships emerging from flame to land where they would. Everyone stood there like lemmings, silent, when you stepped off those creepy things. I saw it on the news, in the streets. *It wasn't normal*."

Exactly! I felt it in my very marrow at that moment those words crossed my lips. It wasn't fucking normal! It wasn't normal, yet we all acted as if it was.

Phi, muscled arms wound around my middle, rubbed his cheek to mine. It was smooth and lovely. It smelled of fresh air and stiff breezes. Of open places outside of city smog.

I took a greater inhale than I had of my cigarette and let it linger just as long in my lungs.

Engulfed by the man breathing at my ear, *cradled*, being treated more sweetly than any living human had ever treated me, my alarm deflated.

I even offered a conciliatory nod when he reasonably explained, "Your film industry has conditioned you to think extraterrestrials only seek out Earth to invade, steal your resources, and commit genocide."

"Not true." His words should not have been amusing, but I smirked as if he'd struck the perfect chord. "The alien species in the original *Star Trek* were all go go-dancing sluts for Kirk."

"I enjoy the fact that you are humorous." Phi smoothed his fingers over my sex-tangled curls, tugging playfully to watch a spiral bounce back, and in a way that gave inexplicable pleasure. Then I was enfolded again. Brushing my ear, his lips parted to impart more sweet words. "It was fortuitous that I found you first, Emily."

Strangeways can be found at all major online retailers.

Addison Cain

USA TODAY bestselling author and Amazon Top 25 bestselling author, Addison Cain is best known for her dark romances, smoldering paranormal suspense, and twisted alien worlds. Her antiheroes are not always redeemable, her lead females stand fierce, and nothing is ever as it seems.

Deep and sometimes heart wrenching, her books are not for the faint of heart. But they are just right for those who enjoy unapologetic bad boys, aggressive alphas, and a hint of violence in a kiss.

Visit her website: addisoncain.com

Don't miss these exciting titles by Addison Cain!

Strangeways

The Golden Line

The Alpha's Claim Series:
Born to be Bound
Born To Be Broken
Reborn
Stolen
Corrupted (coming soon)

Wren's Song Series:
Branded

Silenced

The Irdesi Empire Series:
Sigil
Sovereign
Que (coming soon)

Cradle of Darkness Series:
Catacombs
Cathedral
The Relic

A Trick of the Light Duet:
A Taste of Shine
A Shot in the Dark

Historical Romance:
Dark Side of the Sun

Horror:
The White Queen
Immaculate

CPSIA information can be obtained
at www.ICGtesting.com
Printed in the USA
LVHW050434050720
659748LV00005B/331